Kids Love Reading
Choose Your Own Adventure®!

"I felt like I was in the story!"
Bridan Merrill, age 9

"I LOVE *Choose Your Own Adventure* books because I take risks but if something bad happens I don't actually have something bad happen to me."
Eli Askew, age 8

"I love the books. They're so fun. You are the character, you choose your adventure!"
Josslyn Jewett, age 8

"I liked it when I got off a boat and there was a sausage bus and I got in and...I shouldn't tell you any more because it's a secret!"
Liam Prescott, age 8

Illustrated by Vladimir Semionov and Fian Arroyo
Book design: Stacey Boyd, Big Eyedea Visual Design
For information regarding permission, write to:

CHOOSECO

P.O. Box 46, Waitsfield, Vermont 05673
www.cyoa.com

A DRAGONLARK BOOK

Publisher's Cataloging-In-Publication Data
Names: Gilligan, Shannon. | Semionov, Vladimir, illustrator. Arroyo, Fian, illustrator.
Title: Unicorn Princess / by Shannon Gilligan ; illustrated by: Vladimir Semionov and Fian Arroyo.
Other Titles: Choose your own adventure. Dragonlarks.
Description: Waitsfield, Vermont : Chooseco, [2018] | Summary: You and your new friend Jo set out a unicorn on Princess Island during your third year of princess camp, making choices which will determine what will happen next in the story.
Identifiers: ISBN 1-937133-28-1 | ISBN 978-1-937133-28-3
Subjects: LCSH: Princesses—Juvenile fiction. | Camps—Juvenile fiction. | Ghosts—Juvenile fiction. | CYAC: Princesses—Fiction. | Camps—Fiction. | Ghosts—Fiction. | LCGFT: Action and adventure fiction. | Choose-your-own stories.
Classification: LCC PZ7.G414 Prp 2016 | DDC [Fic]—dc23

Published simultaneously in the United States and Canada

Printed in China

13 12 11 10 9 8 7 6 5 4

CHOOSE YOUR OWN ADVENTURE®

Unicorn Princess

BY SHANNON GILLIGAN
WITH ELIZABETH MIDDLEMAN

ILLUSTRATED BY VLADIMIR SEMIONOV
AND FIAN ARROYO

A DRAGONLARK BOOK

To all of the little princesses out there,
but especially to Suzy, Lila, and Avery.

With thanks and love to Queens Barbara and
Valerie, and his royal highness, Robert.

And to MJM and RAM.

READ THIS FIRST!!!

WATCH OUT!
THIS BOOK IS DIFFERENT
from every book you've ever read.

Do not read this book from the first page
through to the last page.
Instead, start on page 1 and read until you
come to your first choice. Then turn to the
page shown and see what happens.

When you come to the end of a story,
you can go back and start again.
Every choice leads to a new adventure.

Good luck!

"Bye Mom! Bye Dad!" you yell as you pull your trunk down the dock.

"Have a great summer, Peregrine," your dad, King Edward, says, blowing you a kiss.

"Straighten your tiara, sweetheart," your mom, Queen Helena, adds, waving.

You wave back at your parents. Your name is Princess Peregrine Yvette, but everyone calls you Perri. This is your third summer at Princess Island Camp. You are finally old enough to wear the junior camper outfit. Looking down you notice your skort is already wrinkled. *Maybe it's just better to have a messy uniform on the first day,* you think. You continue down to the end of the dock to the welcome table. You look around for friends, but you don't see anyone you know.

Turn to the next page.

Your best friend, Crown Princess Caroline, is not coming back.

She wrote you about it this past winter.

"Mom, it just won't be the same without Caroline," you'd whined.

"I know it must feel that way, Perri," your mom had said, "but who knows what this year will bring? Duchess Anastasia and I did not meet until our third year at camp. Remember the beautiful compass she sent for your ninth birthday?"

"You met Aunt Anastasia at Princess Island?"

"I did! And we have been best friends ever since," your mom had answered. "So chin up."

Go on to the next page

You arrive at the Princess Island welcome table and perform a perfect curtsy with your head dipped. (You've been practicing.) But when you look up, you see a senior counselor instead of Head of Camp.

"Where is Mrs. Wiggins?" you ask, puzzled. As the counselor answers, a huge gust of wind rises off the lake. All the welcome packets *whoosh* up into the air and fall in the water. Most of them get soaked! Luckily, one landed on the dock. It reads: "Josefina Fernanda De Las Flores, Trout Lily, Age 9."

Trout Lily is your cabin too!

Turn to the next page.

Josefina must be a new camper. A bunch of senior counselors scramble to gather and dry the wet envelopes. Where is Mrs. Wiggins? You need to find her before more things go wrong.

If you decide to find Josefina and give her the welcome packet, turn to page 7.

If you decide to go in search of Mrs. Wiggins, turn to page 32.

You approach a senior counselor near the boats. You wave the only dry welcome packet at her. Her name tag says "Emily."

"Emily, I need to get this to a new girl," you explain. "Can you . . ."

Emily turns her head, raising a finger to signal "give me a sec."

"Fred, we need you at check-in. Mrs. Wiggins is not here . . . and we are going to need all new welcome packets," she announces into her walkie-talkie.

Whoosh, buzz, beep. "Roger that," Fred's voice booms out of the walkie-talkie. "Over."

Emily rolls her eyes.

"I need to find Josefina Fernanda De Las Flores," you pipe up.

"I think she's already on the island. Hop in," Emily says, pointing to a small Zodiac boat.

You and Emily zoom to Princess Island in a flash.

Turn to the next page.

8

Emily drops you and your gear at the main dock and waves as she pulls away. You spot a girl sitting alone on a small, old trunk under a chestnut tree. She has long, jet black curls pulled up in a high ponytail and tiny sequins at the corners of her eyes. She wears the same skort and polo that you're wearing.

"Are you," you begin, looking down to check the long name, "Josefina Fernanda De Las Flores?"

"Yes. Call me Jo," she answers.

"Hi Jo, I'm Perri. I have your welcome packet," you say. You hand Jo the envelope and curtsy. "There was an accident on the mainland and all the rest went into the water."

"Thanks so much," she replies, curtsying back like a pro. She looks at the packet. "Do you know where Trout Lily is?"

"I sure do. Follow me," you say with a smile.

Turn to page 11

You lead Jo through the woods to Trout Lily. You un into several counselors along the way. You also sk everyone if they have seen Mrs. Wiggins.

"Funny," says Cassandra Smythe, "I haven't seen her yet."

"Me either," Lady Antonia Cadwell adds. "Sorry."

When you learn that Jo is an expert rider, you nake a quick detour to the barns.

"Sammy is my favorite horse," you say.

Sammy suddenly lets out a loud fart!

You both giggle and say in unison, "Pardon YOU, Miss Sammy!"

Turn to page 46.

12

"A unicorn!" gasps Jo.

"So you saw it too!" you answer.

Jo nods excitedly. "Let me hide this," she says, pointing at her trunk. "It will be safe here. As long as it stays shut and nothing gets out," she adds.

"G-g-gets out?" you stammer. "What do you mean?"

"Oh . . . nothing," Jo shrugs. "Come on. Let's go unicorn hunting." She starts into the woods. But just then, three loud gongs sound over the loudspeakers.

"Three gongs mean it's lunch," you explain. "If we don't get there on time, we could get demerits."

Jo laughs. "And I don't want to do that on the first day!" Then she stops, frowning. "But what about my trunk?"

If you tell Jo her trunk will be safe wher it is, and to go straight to lunch turn to page 27

If you ask Jo why she is s worried about the trunk turn to page 33

"Jo, I think I just saw a . . ."

". . . a unicorn?" Jo asks, finishing your sentence.

"Come on!" you cry, running off the path.

"Yay!" Jo says, right behind you. You both scramble through the woods. But when you reach the tree, the unicorn is gone.

And the tree looks completely normal.

"What happened to the green glow?" Jo asks.

"You saw it too!" you say.

"Let's come back later. I need to put this trunk away," Jo says. You notice she sounds a little nervous when she mentions the trunk.

Turn to the next page.

14

When you get to Trout Lily, the cabin is empty. Jo carefully places the trunk beside her cubby. She triple checks that the latches are latched and gives you a thumbs-up.

"What's in there?" you ask.

"I . . . I can't tell," Jo says, blushing. "But it's best to stay away from it."

"Perrrrri? Are you there?" someone hollers from outside.

"Pandora!" you exclaim, rushing to hug her.

"Hello, you must be Miss Josefina. Or Jo, right?" Pandora winks.

Jo curtsies and nods. "It is such a pleasant pleasure to be meeting you," she says.

Turn to page 16

Three gongs sound over the loudspeaker.

"You girls ready to head to lunch?" Pandora asks.

"We were actually going to look for Jo's . . . lost, umm . . ." you stammer.

". . . dance costume," Jo blurts. "I don't know how I lost it. We were going to backtrack past the stables.

You look at Pandora, then at Jo. You've never told a lie before—not that you remember; well, maybe a few fibs . . .

If you decide to change the subjec
to get out of Jo's fik
turn to page 19

If you go along with Jo's story
turn to page 30

You arrive soaked to the Arts and Crafts building. But Mrs. Wiggins is not there either.

Where could Mrs. Wiggins be? you wonder, sneezing twice. "We better go to the nurse," you tell o.

The nurse at the infirmary gives you a cozy blanket, ome hot soup, and a dose of Vitamin C. You drift ff to sleep and dream about winning the Cabin Cup. Mrs. Wiggins is there, and your mom and dad, even Harold.

You wake up facing your favorite yellow bear. The urse must have pulled it from your backpack. It's rom when you were a little kid. But you still bring it o camp.

You hug Yellow Baby and notice someone on the ed next to you.

Turn to page 42.

"I'm really hungry," you announce. "Do you mind if we look for the dance costume later?"

"Sure," Jo says.

The three of you head to the Main Lodge.

As soon as you finish eating, you whisper to Jo, "Do you know Princess Egg Latin?"

She nods.

In your secret language you say, "Wegg-ee can egg-earch fegg-or the y-egg-ou kn-egg-ow wh-egg-at egg-o-negg-ight. Bring your flashlight."

Jo replies, "Egg-I wasn't jegg-o-kegging about my dance cegg-ostegg-ume. It's the perfect disguise. And I have *extras*."

Turn to page 21.

You go back to Trout Lily, unpack your trunks, make your bunks, and have a water fight.

"Three demerits for Trout Lily!" Pandora barks.

Even if she is your friend, Pandora is strict.

Finally, it's lights out. Once you hear a few snores, you peek to make sure everyone is asleep. Jo is already up, putting on her dance costume. She tiptoes over to your bed, handing you a matching outfit.

"I knew these would come in handy," she whispers.

"Did you get the flashlights?" you ask, quickly pulling on the costume.

"Check."

"I've got my lucky compass. Let's go."

Turn to the next page.

You follow the compass toward the magic tree. The tree is glowing again. When you are a few feet away, you see its trunk *is* a real, living, talking face!

"Hello, Miss Tree," you say.

"Hello, to you, too, Missss . . . whoooo?" the tree responds.

"My name is Princess Peregrine Yvette," you say.

"And I'm Princess Josefina," Jo says. "Call me Jo."

"It is a fine pleasure to be acquainted, Your Royalties," the tree bellows.

"We are looking for a unicorn, have you seen her?" you ask.

"Yes, of course, the unicorn drinks at this pond every day," she says, pointing with a low branch to a small pond nearby. "Would you like me to call for her?"

"Yes please, Miss Tree," you say.

Turn to page 25

Miss Tree's roots burst with green and blue light, down through the forest floor. Leaves *whoosh* around you as a gust of wind swirls through the air.

In an instant, the unicorn appears.

You and Jo curtsy deeply, in awe of the beautiful unicorn. The unicorn's horn lights up.

The unicorn bends one knee. You hop onto her back and reach down to pull Jo up. You may have reached Experienced Horseback Riding last summer, but Jo is an Expert. She takes the unicorn's mane with confidence. You hold on tight as the unicorn lifts up into the air, flying over the Princess Island woods.

Princess Island has never looked so beautiful!

The End

"Your trunk will be safe here. Besides, unicorns arely show their horns during daylight. We have a etter chance of finding her tonight," you tell Jo.

"You're right," Jo agrees. "Also, I'm starving."

You hurry to the Main Lodge for lunch. You spend ne whole day mapping out your path to the unicorn.

That night, you both search all night for the nicorn, and she is nowhere to be found. All that you nd is a creepy, shuttered cabin.

Going inside, you find that everything inside the abin is actually brand new! There is an old-style nusic machine playing all different sorts of music om around the world. Jo fishes out lots of dazzling ance outfits for you both to wear.

She teaches you the merengue, the polka, how to allroom dance, and even how to square dance!

Turn to the next page.

You and Jo sneak out to the cabin every chance you get all summer, practicing your dance routine for the pageant at the Princess Play-offs. A few times you get demerits for sleeping through horseback riding. Another time, you mix glue with the paint in crafts. Your mind is on your dance routine!

After hours and hours of practice, it is finally time for the pageant. You wear a beautiful costume with wings covered in sequins. Jo put sequins at the corners of your eyes too, just like she had on the first day of camp.

Peeking from behind the curtain, you wave to your parents in the crowd. Your brother Prince Harold is here too.

The music cues and the curtain opens. You and Jo dance better than you ever have! You even get a standing ovation.

After the show, Mrs. Wiggins tells you and Jo, "That was the best dance routine in camp history!" She gives you both a bouquet of roses and a big hug.

For the first time, you are in the running for Top Princess!

The End

"Okay, good luck finding it!" Pandora says. "See you at the lodge."

"Did you really lose your dance costume?" you ask Jo.

"Not exactly. But it was the only thing I could think of. Let's find the unicorn," Jo says.

You set out into the woods. You don't find the unicorn, but you do have fun. You head back to Trout Lily. You are bunking above another new camper, Princess Ava Siobhan, and you introduce yourselves.

Junior counselor Lady Osgood throws a s'mores party under the stars. You, Jo, Ava, and your other cabinmates laugh and sing camp songs until bedtime.

Turn to page 55

You walk over to the senior counselor. Her name tag says "Emily."

"Hi Emily, can you take me over to Princess Island? I need to find Mrs. Wiggins," you say.

"I'm strictly dock duty," Emily says. She's no help.

Scanning the dock, you see your brother, Harold. He's a counselor this year at Prince Island.

Harold is standing with a group of younger boys. These must be his campers. He is reading something from a clipboard.

"Hey! Harold! I need your help," you yelp, running over and waving your arms.

Harold rolls his eyes as if he's the funniest person in the whole world. "What have you got yourself into this time, 'Princess Dirt'?" he asks.

Turn to page 37

"Let's take a shortcut," you say, grabbing your lucky compass out of your pocket and leading Jo toward the tree.

"What's in your trunk, anyway?" you ask.

But Jo changes the subject. She tells you about dancing, her snot-nosed brother over on Prince Island, and the horses she loves back home.

"Oh my gosh, it's getting late. I lost track of time!" you say.

"I was thinking the same thing," Jo says. "Let's look for the unicorn later."

"I agree," you say. "I haven't eaten since breakfast, and it must be almost dinner!"

You check your compass and head in the direction of the Main Lodge.

Turn to the next page.

When you enter the Main Lodge, someone calls your name.

"Perri! Jo! Where have you girls been?" Mrs. Wiggins asks. "We found your trunks near the stables and have been looking for you both ever since."

"My trunk!" Jo squeaks.

Go on to the next page

"Don't worry. Your trunks are stowed in your cabin. But I'm afraid we're going to have to give you both five demerits for disappearing like that."

"Sorry Mrs. Wiggins," you say. "It's my fault. I should take Jo's demerits. I lost track of time using my new compass."

"I'm just happy that you're both safe," Mrs. Wiggins replies.

Turn to the next page.

The first dinner of the summer is always a feast. You eat fried chicken, hamburgers, corn on the cob, and green salad. Dessert is banana splits followed by a huge sing-along at the bonfire on the beach. You are so tired when you get back to Trout Lily, Pandora, the cabin counselor, gives you and Jo permission to unpack your trunks first thing in the morning.

Turn to page 49

"I don't have time for this, Prince Claptrap!" you
reply. His campers try not to laugh.

"All of the welcome packets just blew into the
water. I found this one, and I need to locate Josefina
something or other."

Harold's eyes spring open. He picks up his walkie-
talkie. *Whoosh, buzz, beep.* "We have a situation at
the dock. I'll be making a detour at Princess Island."

Looking around, Harold waves to Emily. "Hey!
Emily, I need you to watch my campers for a few
minutes."

"Fine with me!" Emily yells back, and the crowd of
younger boys waddle over to Emily, dragging their
suitcases.

You hear over the walkie-talkie, "Roger that. Be
careful out there. Water's looking choppy. Over and
out."

You and Harold leap into the boat and take off for
Princess Island.

Turn to the next page.

You squeeze Josefina's welcome packet to your chest and grab on to the gunwale of the boat. *Uh-oh.* The choppy water makes you feel sick to your stomach. You start slowly counting backward from twenty. It's one of the tricks your dad taught you for warding off seasickness.

Harold maneuvers the boat better than you thought he could. Only a little bit of water has splashed over the sides. But the clouds overhead swirl and turn dark gray. Princess Island still looks like a tiny speck.

CRACK! BOOM!

You see lightning and hear thunder in the distance.

"Ten Mississippi . . . nine Mississippi . . . eight Mississippi . . ." you chant, breathing slowly and trying to look brave.

"We're almost there!" Harold shouts. "Hold on tight!"

Turn to the next page.

Just as you finish your count and raindrops start falling from the sky, you and Harold arrive safely at the Princess Island shore.

"Thank you, Harold. You saved me, and the summer," you say.

"You're my sister, even if you can be a pill," he says, giving you a little shove. "I think I'll go grab some food from the Main Lodge. Good luck finding what's her name, Dirt."

Harold ties up the boat and leaves you on the dock. There's no one in sight. Everyone must be inside.

Grabbing your trunk and Josefina's welcome packet, you make your way to Trout Lily.

Go on to the next page

On a shortcut through the woods, you see a girl sitting all alone holding her face in her palms.

"Hey, are you okay?" you ask.

Sniffling, she answers, "I'm Jo. I'm new here, and I don't know where to go."

"Jo, as in, Josefina?"

She nods, wiping her nose and starting to smile.

Holding the welcome packet out proudly, you say, "I have your welcome packet!"

"You do?" Jo squeals. "Wow!"

"Want to help me find Mrs. Wiggins, the head of camp?"

"Sure! Sounds fun."

You and Jo drop your things at Trout Lily. Then you head to the Main Lodge. Mrs. Wiggins is not in her office or the dining room. You check everywhere.

"Let's try Arts and Crafts," you suggest.

"But it's raining really hard," Jo says. "Nanny Tempers told me never stay out in the rain."

"Nannies don't know everything!" you holler back, as you run ahead.

Turn to page 17.

"Mrs. Wiggins!" you yelp, jumping up. "I have been looking for you!"

"I'm so happy to see you, Perri," Mrs. Wiggins says with a big smile. "I hope that you didn't get sick out in the rain."

You blush. "Maybe a little bit," you stammer, rushing to curtsy.

"Never mind that, you stay in bed," Mrs. Wiggins says. She gives you a big hug. Mrs. Wiggins' tummy is the size of a watermelon. She's having a baby!

"Is it going to be a boy or girl?" you ask.

"A girl," Mrs. Wiggins smiles. "And I was thinking her name should be Peregrine."

"Then I want new baby Peregrine to have Yellow Baby," you say, handing her your treasured bear.

"Why, thank you, Perri," Mrs. Wiggins says. "This is very kind. You have grown up into a great princess." She studies Yellow Baby, who is worn with love, and smiles at you. "Peregrine, you keep Yellow Baby safe with you," she says. "For just a little while longer."

The End

When you are away from the other campers, Jo turns to you. "Can you keep a secret?" she asks.

"Promise," you say.

"You know that old trunk I brought to camp?" she asks.

You nod.

Go on to the next page

"Well, it had a ghost inside. And I think it . . . got out."

"A *ghost?!*" you cry.

"Shhh!" Jo replies.

If you say, "We better tell Mrs. Wiggins right away before the ghost attacks the whole camp!" turn to page 50.

If you decide to keep Jo's little ghost problem a secret, turn to page 77.

Leaving the stables, you notice a strange tree in the woods. It's glowing. You squint your eyes. There's a pattern on its trunk that juts and smooths to form a face. Standing right in front of it is a tall, beautiful horse.

Wait, that's not a horse. It's a unicorn!
You are about to dash into the woods when you remember Jo. She doesn't have any friends yet. You don't want to leave her all alone.

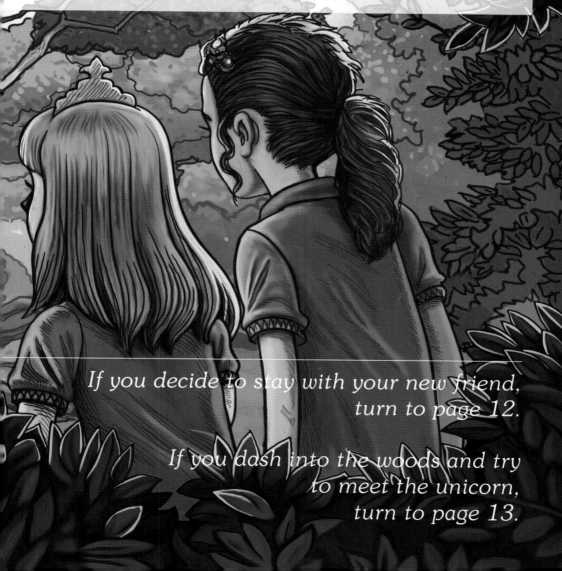

If you decide to stay with your new friend, turn to page 12.

If you dash into the woods and try to meet the unicorn, turn to page 13.

"Psst. Perri. Wake up," someone says, shaking your arm.

"Jo? What is it?" you ask, sitting up. You look around. Something isn't right.

Your camp uniforms are neatly folded on the shelves. Your riding boots, soccer cleats, water shoes, and sandals are neatly lined up in a row.

"Did you unpack?" you ask Jo.

She shakes her head no.

"This isn't my tiara," Princess Ava, another new girl, mumbles.

"Is this it? I'm not sure why it's in the trash can," your cousin, Lady Millicent, offers.

"Where is my toothbrush?" Lady Eunice Pettigrew wonders, rustling through her things. "All I can find is this smelly, rotten . . . *fish!*" she shrieks, throwing a wriggling fish into the air. Ava and Millicent scream.

"Uh-oh," Jo says, suddenly pale. She motions you to follow her outside.

Turn to page 44.

"Jo, we need to report the ghost," you say.

"I have a book of spells in my trunk. Can we try that first?"

"Okay. Quickly. Then we should tell Mrs. Wiggins."

Jo runs to her trunk and finds the book of spells. She leafs through its pages.

Something flies past your head. It looks like a see-through white bat. But it's the ghost! "Whoa! Hey there! Ghost! What's your name?" you cry.

Go on to the next page

The ghost freezes and slowly floats down to meet you.

"You can see me?" he asks.

"Of course I can see you," you say. "I'm Perri."

"My name is Theo. No one ever talks to me. That's why I play tricks. All I want is a friend. Will you be my friend?"

Turn to the next page.

"Sure," you reply. "But I can only be friends with kids and ghosts with manners. And stealing is not good manners. It's also not very nice," you say.

"You're right," Theo says. "I'm sorry. I just wanted to be out of the trunk having fun at camp. Just like you."

Jo motions for you to come over to her. She points to a spell called "RETURN TO THE TRUNK."

You feel sad for Theo the ghost. Who wants to be cooped up in a trunk all day? But how do you know that Theo will stay on good behavior and not keep messing with people's things?

If you point to the spell, and nod at Jo go on to the next page

If you decide to give Theo a chance and let him stay at camp as long as he behaves turn to page 57

Jo nods back. The two of you read aloud in unison:

Apples and pears are perfect for pie,
Ghosts you meet are likely to lie,
Pumpkins are sweet,
But not very deep,
Now go . . . back . . . to . . . sleep.

Before you know it, Theo drifts to Earth and starts to snore. You huff and puff him over to Jo's trunk. (You can't actually grab a ghost. There is nothing to grab.) He snuggles inside, and Jo snaps the trunk shut.

"Let's put this someplace where no one can find it," Jo says.

"I know just the place," you say. "Follow me."

The End

You spend the night tossing and turning. You are worried about Mrs. Wiggins. Where is she? Finally, you get out of bed and set off for Prince Island with your compass. *I'll go talk to Harold,* you think. He may be a dweeb, but he is still your brother.

There's a one-person kayak in the boathouse. You pull it off the rack and set out across the water. You hold your lucky compass between your two big toes, using it to guide you in the right direction and to light the way.

Turn to the next page.

CLONK! Something hits the bottom of your kayak. And then another, *clonk!* Followed by a *thud.*

You look around and nothing's there.

"Hello?" you say.

"Hey! Watch where you're rowing, pip-squeak!" you hear.

"Who's there?" you ask the darkness.

"The name's Betti, Betti Splendi," the voice answers.

You feel a little splash and, looking down, see a bright magenta fish sparkling in the moonlight.

Turn to page 59

"Jo, Theo is right. We can't keep him in a box all summer!" you say.

Jo closes the book of spells. "But how do we know that he won't cause more trouble?"

"I'll fix everything!" Theo chirps.

That night, you and Theo have the first of many nightly chats. You soon become fast friends.

Who would think a ghost could be so good at tidying up Trout Lily? Not to mention hosting tea parties.

When you win Neatest Cabin at the end of the summer, everyone agrees, it's mostly thanks to Theo!

The End

"Wow!" you say. "I've never met a fish that could talk. Do you know the way to Prince Island?"

"Follow me!" Betti says, shooting an electric wave of light up her spine and down her fins.

Staying close (but not too close) to Betti, you paddle to Prince Island. As you pull your kayak onto the sand, Betti's glow dims.

"Thank you, Betti, for all of your help," you say.

"No sweat, pip-squeak," Betti says, splashing you again with her back fin.

Looking past Betti, you see flashing lights coming from Princess Island. Is that Morse code? Grabbing a stick, you translate the message in the sand.

Turn to the next page.

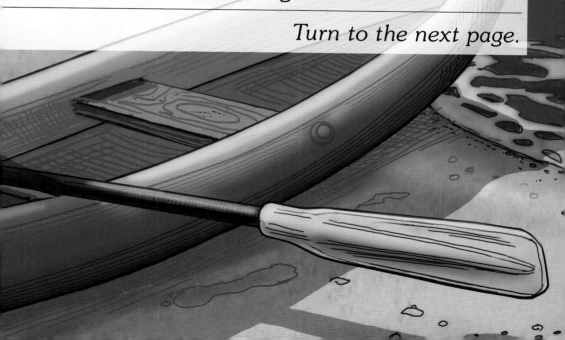

You step back and read the message out:

FOLLOW THE NORTH STAR WEST. 911.

The lights across the water keep blinking the same message over and over. You might be the only person awake to see it.

"Sounds like trouble," Betti says. "I say we swim over and investigate!"

If you decide to head back to Princess Island go on to the next page

If you decide to follow Betti turn to page 62

If you decide to find Harold, and say goodbye to Betti for now turn to page 69

"Betti, I need to go back," you say. "I'm in trouble already."

"Okay. I'll check out the call for help," she says.

You are about to jump back into your kayak when the head counselor appears. *What's the head counselor of Princess Island doing here?* you wonder.

"Hey, who's there?" she shouts, shining a bright light in your eyes.

"It's me . . . Princess Perri," you gulp. "Third summer, Princess Island camper."

"What are you doing out at this hour Princess Perri? Campers should be asleep in their cabins," she says.

"I . . . I . . . I couldn't sleep, so I paddled over here to see my brother, Harold," you say. Words and tears pour out.

"Your *brother?*" she says. She begins to fade. "Wrong island, kiddo."

You sit up. The sun is rising. All your bunkmates are asleep. You are in your own bunk.

It was all a dream! And it's the first day of the whole summer on Princess Island!

The End

"Let's go take a look and see if we can help."

Betti's fins burst with rainbow beams of light as she swims happily toward the cove. The sun is starting to peek through the clouds just as Betti gives you another little splash to say "we're here."

You push quietly through the marshes, gliding close behind Betti's back fin. Cicadas and bush crickets chirp. Fireflies blink like shooting stars. You feel so happy!

Other fish join you. They all blink in gorgeous colors. They look like they are talking underwater.

"Here's the problem," Betti announces, shooting some neon blue sparks as she swims up alongside your kayak. The other fish have followed her.

"Renata," Betti continues, "she's a parrot fish, is caught behind some rocks near shore. Not sure how she swam in there. Can you help move the rocks so she can escape?"

"I'd be happy to," you reply.

Turn to page 64

Betti leads you to Renata, a beautiful coral-pink fish with long green fins, stuck behind a few large rocks.

"Here you go, Renata," you say, gently lifting a rock to create an escape route.

Renata darts out into the larger lake and jumps with joy. All the fish swim and frisk about. They send light beams of thanks.

Turn to page 67.

You even spot a blue mermaid as she climbs onto a nearby rock and waves at you.

"Kee-k-cluck-eeee, eee, eee," she says. "That means, 'I love you,'" she explains.

Climbing back into your kayak, you wave goodbye to these magical beings.

"I'll miss you very much! And I will be back again soon," you say. "Kee-k-cluck-eee, eee, eee!"

The End

"Good luck, Betti!" you say. "I have to go see my brother Harold right now."

You wave goodbye to the magical fish and walk down a path toward the circle of Prince Island cabins, arranged around the campfire. It's starting to get light out. Two counselors are pulling the Prince Island flag up the flagpole. Four long gongs sound over the loudspeaker. It's the wake-up bell.

You hide behind a tree trunk, to look around. Harold walks out of his cabin, heading toward what must be the Prince Island Main Lodge.

You shuffle through the trees.

"Psst," you whisper loudly.

"Huh," Harold looks around, confused.

"Harold, it's me, Perri," you say.

"Dirt? What are you doing here?"

Turn to the next page.

"Perri? Is everything okay? You shouldn't be over here," Harold says.

"I couldn't sleep," you say, walking out from behind the tree. "I don't know where Mrs. Wiggins is Everything is going wrong. I told Pandora a fib. I feel bad." Tears well up in your eyes as you say, "I don't think I'll ever be a good princess let alone a good queen."

Harold gestures for you to sit down on the bench, and you do.

Go on to the next page

"Was it a lie or just a fib?" Harold asks.

"A fib," you answer.

"Well, you should always tell the truth," Harold ays, "but everyone makes mistakes. And don't worry o much about being a good princess. Just be Perri, nd you'll turn out just fine."

Turn to the next page.

"Now I should get you back across the lake," Harold says.

"Before we go, I have a question," you say. "Harold, have you ever heard a fish talk?"

"Oh. Have you met Betti?" Harold asks.

"You know about Betti?" you say.

"I'm older than you. I know more than you think. Betti brings messages back and forth between the two camps! Look for a note tonight in your cabin sink. Which cabin are you in?"

"Trout Lily," you say.

"The middle sink. Tonight. Don't forget," Harold whispers. Harold loads your kayak into a Prince Island boat and drives you back to Princess Island. Everyone is just getting up. You are able to sneak back to Trout Lily without being caught.

Go on to the next page

That day you are groggy, but you feel better. And that night, you wait all night by the middle sink. Just when you are about to fall asleep from boredom, a note pops up through the stopper. *Plink!*

Harold must have used special waterproof paper because the ink didn't run at all.

The note says: AVA WILL KNOW.

Ava will know *what?*

You tiptoe through the cabin, making sure to miss the squeaky floorboards, and tap Ava on the shoulder.

She blinks awake and smiles.

"It's about time," she whispers.

As she crawls out of bed, you can see she is dressed like a zebra!

"Here," she says, handing you your costume.

You pull on the brown, yellow, and white clothes, and then finally, beautiful, multicolored wings that you wear on your back and arms like a cape.

You are a bumblebee!

Turn to the next page.

You set off into the night and try out your wings.
They work!
    Buzzing at top speed, you zoom through the clouds
batting your wings.

Below, you see Ava galloping at top speed. You follow her trail through the dense trees. She is headed right for the tree you saw on your first day, the one with a trunk that looked like a face.

Ava stops in front of the tree and whistles a loud OOOWWEEEEE.

You dive down until you are hovering right near the tree. Then you flutter the rest of the way to the forest floor. Ava transforms back into Ava, and you transform back into yourself.

Turn to the next page.

The tree twists and creaks and comes to life! She smiles and shakes her leaves like hair.

"It is so nice to see you again, Princess Ava and Princess Perri," the tree says.

Ava curtsies before speaking. "Hello, Miss Tree. We are looking for a magical unicorn."

Your eyes nearly pop out of your head.

"Indeed," Miss Tree responds. "Perri, do you have your compass?"

You pull your lucky compass from a fold in your wings.

"I do," you reply.

"West of the North Star is that-away," Miss Tree points.

Turn to page 78

"I think we should keep this quiet, but what do we do with a ghost for the whole summer?" you ask. "Especially one who likes to cause trouble."

"Good point," Jo agrees.

The sweetest voice you have ever heard speaks out of nowhere. "I can take care of the ghost if you like."

You and Jo whirl around.

It's the unicorn!

Turn to page 83.

You and Ava follow the compass to a clearing. A house ten stories high looms above your head. The windows flash with light. *Crash! Bang! Boom!*

Squeezing Ava's hand tightly, you walk into the house. A ghost is sitting at a table covered with bubbling flasks. Popcorn is bouncing—*pop, pop, pop*—under the lid of a pot on the stove.

The ghost squints and throws papers all over the room. He is making a huge mess on purpose!

You run to the stove and turn off the burner.

"I am Her Royal Highness Princess Peregrine Yvette of Chittenden Palace," you announce. "And this must stop at once."

"But, I can help you find the unicorn! You will just need to solve this riddle," the ghost replies.

"We may only be princesses in training, but we're pretty smart," you say. "Ask me your hardest riddle."

"Okay, smarty-pants Princess. Here's the riddle," the ghost says.

Turn to page 80

"Two camels were facing in opposite directions. One was facing east and one was facing west. They were in the desert so there was no reflection. How can they manage to see each other without walking around or turning around or moving their heads?"

You pull out your lucky compass, inspecting it for clues.

Go on to the next page

Holding the compass up, you swivel around until the needle points exactly east. "Ava! Go stand exactly where I'm pointing."

Ava scurries across the room, standing next to a large dining room hutch. Its drawers and doors are opening and closing, rattling all of the plates and silverware inside. "Now what?" Ava asks you.

Squeezing your compass with a big smile, you turn to the ghost. "I've got it! The camels were facing each other the whole time!"

The ghost is stunned. "That's right. A deal's a deal."

The ghost swirls the flask faster than light, and before you know it, a unicorn appears!

"I always knew unicorns were real!" you say, giving her a big hug.

The End

"Ghosts love unicorns. I'm sure your ghost would
e very happy with us deep in the woods," she adds.
My name is Lena, by the way."

"Hello, Miss Lena," you say.

"Miss Lena Unicorn," Jo adds. You both curtsy
leeply.

"Why there's your ghost now," Lena says softly.

You watch as a white mist floats straight through
he wall of Trout Lily. It looks like a bat wearing a
ong cloak.

"Are you a *real* unicorn?" the ghost asks.

"Yes," Lena says. "And you're invited to spend the
whole summer on Princess Island with us unicorns."

The ghost grabs Lena's sparkling purple mane. The
unicorn rises slowly to the treetops and flies off.

You look at Jo. Jo looks at you.

"There's more than one unicorn?" Jo asks.

"Of course," you reply. "Just part of another
magical summer on Princess Island!"

The End

ABOUT THE ARTISTS

Vladimir Semionov was born in August 1964 in the Republic of Moldavia, of the former USSR. He is a graduate of the Fine Arts Collegium in Kishinev, Moldavia, as well as the Fine Arts Academy of Romania, where he majored in graphics and painting, respectively. He has exhibitions all over the world, in places like Japan and Switzerland, and is currently the Art Director of the SEM&BL Animacompany animation studio in Bucharest, Romania.

Fian Arroyo, with his creative mind and quick draw, has been creating award-winning illustrations and character designs for his clients, including many Fortune-500 companies, in the advertising, editorial, toy and game, and publishing markets for over twenty years. What began as something to do until he found out what he wanted to be when he grew up, has blossomed into a full-time detour from getting a "real job." He has had the pleasure of working with companies such as *U.S. News & World Report,* ABC Television Network, KFC, Taco Bell, *The Los Angeles Times,* SC Johnson, the United States Postal Service and many more.
Originally from San Juan, Puerto Rico, Fian grew up traveling the world as a U.S. Army brat. He graduated from Texas State University in 1986 with a BFA in Commercial Art then moved to Miami, Florida, where he began his freelance illustration career. In 2009, he relocated from Miami Beach to the breathtaking mountains of Asheville, North Carolina where he lives with his wife and two kids.

ABOUT THE AUTHORS

 **Shannon Gilligan** began writing fiction for a living after graduating from Williams College in 1981. She has written over fifteen books for children, including eleven in the *Choose Your Own Adventure* series. Her work has been translated into more than twenty languages. Gilligan also spent a lost decade working on story-based video games in the 1990s. Her day job is publisher of Chooseco. She lives in Warren, Vermont.

Elizabeth Middleman received her BA in English from Skidmore College. She has been writing poetry and fiction for over ten years and most recently worked collaboratively on the *Weregirl* trilogy. Elizabeth lives with her husband in rural Vermont where she enjoys gardening, skiing, hiking, and playing tennis. She has traveled widely across the United States and abroad. Among her favorite writers are William Blake, James Tate, and Salman Rushdie. And she never stopped believing in unicorns.

CHECK OFF THE BOOKS THAT YOU HAVE READ FROM THE

CHOOSE YOUR OWN ADVENTURE® DRAGONLARK SERIES

- ☆ Princess Island
- ☆ Princess Perri and the Second Summer
- ☆ Unicorn Princess
- ☆ Your Very Own Robot
- ☆ Your Very Own Robot Goes Cuckoo-Bananas!
- ☆ Gus Vs. The Robot King
- ☆ Dino Lab
- ☆ Dragon Day
- ☆ Search for the Dragon Queen
- ☆ The Lake Monster Mystery
- ☆ Monsters of the Deep
- ☆ Ghost Island
- ☆ Sand Castle

- ☆ Your Grandparents Are Spies
- ☆ Your Grandparents Are Zombies!
- ☆ Your Grandparents Are Ninjas
- ☆ Your Grandparents Are Werewolves
- ☆ Fire!
- ☆ Lost Dog!
- ☆ Space Pup
- ☆ The Haunted House
- ☆ Return To Haunted House
- ☆ Indian Trail
- ☆ Owl Tree
- ☆ Your Purrr-fect Birthday
- ☆ Caravan
- ☆ Mermaid Island
- ☆ Your Baby Unicorn

COLLECT THEM ALL!

GUS

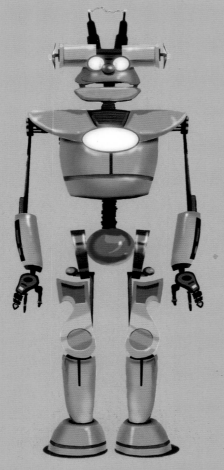

Age: 2

Favorite food:
ice cream

Likes: ice cream,
causing trouble

Dislikes:
junkyards,
water

You can find me in:
Your Very Own Robot
Your Very Own Robot Goes Cuckoo-Bananas
Gus Vs. The Robot King